In The Nick Of Time Too

Praise for In the Nick of Time

"Nick's transformation from a child concerned with material things to a kid who wants to help others rings true.... Mosley's textured cartoon illustrations, which feature painterly backgrounds, ground the story beautifully.... This engaging holiday tale gives children—like the protagonist—a chance to investigate their own privilege."
—KIRKUS REVIEWS

"It's about a boy who saves Christmas - a common enough storyline - but this one is different. After years of collecting children's Christmas books, Deedee Cummings couldn't find (this specific storyline) with a character who looked like her son. She knew how important it was for her son to see a character he could admire.
So she wrote her own."
—USA TODAY

"We all know and understand the importance of seeing oneself in the imagery we're exposed to on a daily basis from the very beginning. As children, we're sponges that inhale information and believe what we're told about ourselves. One way to mold the narrative your children subscribe to is with uplifting, inspiring books that feature faces that look like their own as protagonists."
—ESSENCE

Copyright © 2022 Deedee Cummings

All rights reserved. No part of this book may be reproduced, stored, or transmitted by any means—whether auditory, graphic, mechanical, or electronic—without written permission of both publisher and author, except in the case of brief excerpts used in critical articles and reviews. Unauthorized reproduction of any part of this work is illegal and is punishable by law.

ISBN: 978-1-951218-32-4 (paperback)
ISBN: 978-1-951218-33-1 (ebook)

Because of the dynamic nature of the Internet, any web addresses or links contained in this book may have changed since publication and may no longer be valid. The views expressed in this work are soley those of the author and do not necessarily reflect the views of the publisher, and the publisher hereby disclaims any responsibility for them.

Interior Image Credit: Charlene Mosley

makeawaymedia.com
deedeecummings.com

@makeawaymedia
@authordeedeecummings

Printed in Canada

Other books by the author

Love Is...

Think of it Like This!

My Trip to the Beach

My Dad's Job

Heart

I want to Be a Bennett Belle

If a Caterpillar Can Fly, Why Can't I?

Like Rainwater

In the Nick of Time

This is The Earth

Kayla: A Modern-Day Princess

Kayla: A Modern-Day Princess-- Dishes, Dancing, and Dreams

Kayla: A Modern-Day Princess-- Tough as Tulle

Kayla: A Modern-Day Princess-- These Shoes Are Made for Dancing

Kayla: A Modern-Day Princess-- A Little Magic

Nick and Cooper are best friends. More like brothers, really. They go to the same school, play the same sports, and love the same TV shows.

So, when Cooper asked his mom to spend the night at Nick's house on Christmas Eve, it was a little unusual but not unexpected.

"We won't be opening our presents this year until Christmas evening, so I guess it's okay. As long as it's alright with Nick's parents," Cooper's mom replied.

"It is!" Cooper yelled as he ran off to send Nick a quick text with the good news.

"I'm on my way," he wrote.

"We don't have a bake shop," Nick said. "My mom and dad just bake a lot during the holidays. The whole month of December we make all kinds of cookies and give them to people as gifts. Sometimes my mom even gives them to strangers."

"What kind of cookies?" Cooper asked, more for himself than any other reason. Cooper hoped some of these cookies would be passed his way.

"Chocolate chip, frosted cookies, sugar cookies, gingerbread, snowballs, and these. These are my favorite." Nick pointed to a plate of snickerdoodle cookies. "My mom calls these Nickydoodles."

"Nickydoodles?" Cooper repeated. "I have never heard of those before."

Cooper tasted one of the Nickydoodles and said, "Mmmm. That's delicious!"

"I know, right? That's why they're my favorite!" Nick said. "My mom makes these just for me. NICKYdoodles! They are like snickerdoodles, but they have little bits of toffee in them."

"We are so glad you could make it to our holiday open house!" Nick's dad said as he took everyone's coat to put in the closet.

All of the children came running in, and their eyes grew as wide as Cooper's when he first saw the gigantic table of cookies.

As Cooper watched the kids' excitement, Nick's mom said to him, "I forgot to tell you we are having an open house tonight for our neighbors. We don't all celebrate Christmas, but we all celebrate something. We all believe in love, hope, faith, family, and friendship.

As Nick's family stood at the door to say good night to their last guest, Mrs. Wilson from across the street said that she couldn't remember a better Christmas party in all her life.

"It wasn't just a Christmas party, Mrs. Wilson." Nick's mom reminded her.

"Yes, that's my point," Mrs. Wilson said. "Absolutely nothing has made me believe in the Christmas spirit like sharing stories of hope with others. A celebration of many faiths somehow made my faith stronger and lifted my spirit. Especially the children, what a joy it was to watch them together."

"Ahhh, I understand, Mrs. Wilson. Merry Christmas," Nick's mom said.

"And happy holidays to all!" Mrs. Wilson added.

"Yes, Mrs. Wilson, and happy holidays to all."

As they closed the door, they noticed that Cooper passed out on the couch. Nick's dad said, "He went hard on that nog."

"Will you carry him up to Nick's room?" Nick's mom asked.
"He's 12! And he's fast asleep. He will be fine. If he wakes up, he'll go upstairs." Nick's dad covered Cooper with a blanket.

It was Christmas Eve, and everyone went to sleep knowing that when they woke up, Santa would have already come and gone.

"On Christmas Eve?" Nick asked.

"Yes!" Cooper didn't understand why Nick was not more alarmed.

"And he came through the chimney?"

"Yes! Yes! Yes! Let's get your parents!" Cooper urged.

"Dude, that's Santa," Nick explained.

"But he didn't look like Santa, Nick."

"What did he look like?"

"Well, he had on black boots, and a red suit, a white beard, and a red ha—"

Nick cut Cooper off. "That's Santa!"

"But he's Black," Cooper said.

"My Santa is Black." Nick told Cooper. "You saw Santa."

"I don't think he's Santa. I have never seen a Black Santa."

"Okay, let's talk about this." Nick said calmly. "You believe in Santa?"

"Yes. One hundred percent," Cooper confirmed.

"And you believe that Santa flies all over the world in one night in a sleigh?"

"Yes."

"Pulled by reindeer?" Nick continued.

"Yes."

"Who can fly?"

"Yesssssss."

Nick paused, "But you don't believe Santa can be Black?"

"I said I've never **seen** it. Look man, I've just never thought about it."

"You need to come over here more often," Nick said. "Come on. Let's go see."
"See Santa?" Cooper asked.
"Yes, let's go see Santa." Nick said, as he led the way back downstairs.

To their surprise, Santa was waiting on them with milk and a plate of cookies.

"You boys know I don't usually hang around, but I couldn't help hearing that someone needs a little reassurance." In Santa's comforting way, his eyebrows seemed to rise as his head lowered.

Cooper looked at Nick as if to say, **He knows my name!** Nick shrugged. Neither was very sure what Santa wanted to say.

"Come sit with me, Cooper," Santa encouraged.

Cooper began, "I am so sorry I didn't believe you were Santa. I just didn't know."

"Ahhhh son, you are a great kid. You've done nothing wrong. We are all lifelong learners. That means every day for the rest of your life you will learn something new. Or you should anyway."

"Really? I thought that ended with the 12th grade."

Santa chuckled. "Oh no! Not even a little. You will learn for the rest of your life. The best thing you did today was listen to your best friend. I am so proud of you for that."

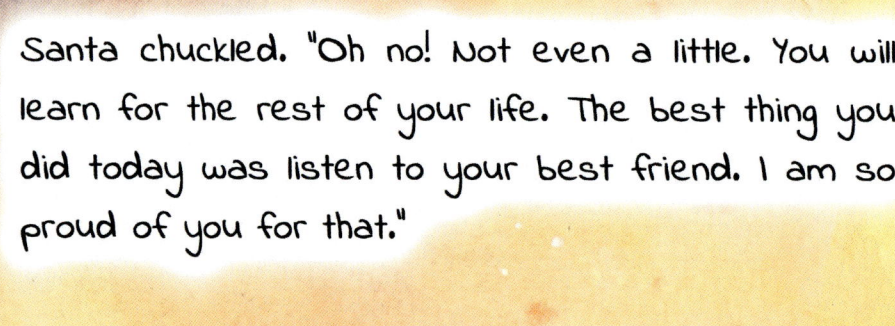

Santa looked at the plate that was once full and said, "Oh my. You two sure do love cookies, don't you? These are my favorite. They are like Snickerdoodles, but they are...."

"Nickydoodles!" Nick could not contain his excitement. He and Santa loved the same cookies!

"Nickydoodles?" Santa asked.

"Or you might want to call them Saint Nickydoodles, Santa."

Santa laughed so hard his tummy shook up and down like a bowl full of jelly. With happy tears in the corners of his eyes, Santa told the boys, "Yes! I love it! Nickydoodles! Named after me and you, Nick Saint. It looks like the plate needs to be filled up again."

Dear Nick and Cooper,
Best friends as close as brothers.
What a joy it was to meet you.
I have a message I need you to share with others.

Don't waste one minute of the day
worrying about things people say about skin or color.
There are more important things to spend time on like,
spreading hope,
and taking care of one another.

I'm so proud of the friendship you have.
And it came in the nick of time that you bonded as brothers.
Santa doesn't care about the color of children.
There are only nice kids on my list.
Naughty is on the other.

Here's what Santa wants to know.
Do you make the world a little better each day?
Spreading kindness wherever you go?
Hope and love are meant for *everyone*,
not just who some say.

The next time someone makes a big deal about
how a person looks or what they might be made of,
tell them that love comes in all shapes and colors.
You've seen Santa,
and you know, **Santa always looks like love.**

The world needs your message of friendship.
The world needs to see it *from you*.
Share your hope and positivity with everyone you know,
so that all of us might one day be, in the Nick of Time too.

Love always,
St. Nick

How To Make Nickydoodles

1) Heat oven to 400°F.
2) Use a beater to mix the butter and shortening together with 1 cup of sugar in large bowl until it looks fluffy. Add the eggs and continue to mix all together with the beater.
3) Mix the flour, cream of tartar, baking soda and salt together.
4) Slowly add the flour mixture to the butter mixture, beating until it is all mixed together.
5) Mix in the toffee bits. You can buy these already in pieces or put the candy bar in a plastic sandwich bag and crush it up with a spoon. You can also use a little more if you like.
6) Put the leftover 1/3 cup of sugar and the cinnamon in a bowl and stir it up till it is mixed together.
7) Shape the dough into balls about one inch big. Roll them in the sugar and cinnamon mix.
8) Place them on an ungreased cookie sheet.
9) Bake 9 to 11 minutes or until they look a little brown around the edges. Then remove them from the oven. Wait five minutes and then move them to a wire rack to cool.
10) Leave some out for Santa if baking these on Christmas Eve!

Ingredients List:

1/2 cup butter (1 stick), softened
1/2 cup shortening
1 1/3 cups sugar, divided as advised
2 eggs
2 3/4 cups all-purpose flour
2 tsps cream of tartar
1 tsp baking soda
1/4 tsp salt
1 cup of toffee candy bars smashed up
2 tsps ground cinnamon

Author
Deedee Cummings

Deedee is an author, therapist, attorney, and mom from Louisville, Kentucky. The books she writes focus on diversity, social justice, and therapeutic skills for children and adults. Her work has been featured in HuffPost, Forbes, NPR, USA Today, Essence Magazine, Psych Central, Well+Good, and The EveryGirl. Deedee is also the founder of Make A Way Media and The Louisville Book Festival. She believes literacy is a fundamental human right. Her work highlights inspiring messages that remind us all it is never too late to begin again. Cummings founded Make A Way Media in 2014 after struggling to find books with characters who looked like her own children and an extreme lack of stories that reflected their life experiences.

Illustrator
Charlene Mosley

Charlene is a German-American fine artist and illustrator based in San Diego with a Bachelor Degree in Art from San Diego State University. She has traveled worldwide to create art and to immerse herself into different cultures. Charlene has illustrated various award-winning books. Creating illustrations for children's books has been one of the artist's favorite things to do. Every time she reads a new manuscript, it gives her imagination the freedom to embark on another colorful journey of exploration and discovory.

"To make a dream become reality and to share that with the world is the funnest job ever".

-Charlene

The Mission of Make A Way Media

Make A Way Media was founded by Deedee Cummings in 2014 and focuses on creating positive and diverse media images and publications. This company is the driving force behind the Kayla series. To date, *Make A Way Media* has successfully supported the creation and publication of eleven diverse books for children.

We are committed to ensuring that all children have access to diverse books because we know that reading develops esteem, efficacy, and empathy in children. *Make A Way Media* has gifted over 1,000 books to homes, families, community centers, churches, and schools that are severely lacking in diverse children's books. In addition to donating hundreds of books each year, *Make A Way Media* is also an active supporter of the *It Pays to Read* program, donating more than 10% of all proceeds to this literacy awareness nonprofit.

It Pays to Read is a program that works with at-risk youth to improve literacy skills because we believe literacy is a fundamental human right. Literacy affects every area of our lives from our capability to apply for a job, read a prescription bottle, or clearly articulate our wants and needs. Reading changes lives. *It Pays to Read* accomplishes these goals through working with kids on improving their behavioral health and soft job skills, while literally paying kids to read. *Make A Way Media* and *It pays to Read* have similar missions in also recognizing that children are far more likely to become engaged in a book, and will continue to read more, when the books have characters who look like them or reflect their experiences.

In the children's publishing industry, books are eight times more likely to feature an animal as the protagonist than a person of color. *Make A Way Media* is not only working to address this divide by creating books that portray diverse characters throughout the story, but also highlighting these characters as leaders. *Kayla: A Modern-Day Princess* shows Black and Brown girls that they can be leaders too and that princesses come in all colors.

It is important to note that books with black and brown characters are not made solely for black and brown children. All children need to read books and see other positive media and imagery as it lessens the divide between cultures, increases our understanding and empathy towards one another, and combats an overdose of steady negative stereotypes and imagery in our daily media exposure.

Meet the Team

This is an #OwnVoices project. This series was written by a Black author and is being illustrated by a Black artist. This is a rare combination.

Even now, we are still battling gatekeepers in the publishing industry who decide what stories are worthy of being told and who will illustrate them. Characters of color are not the only area severely underrepresented; authors and illustrators of color are too.

#OwnVoices is a movement that began on Twitter, but it has now extended far beyond that platform. People of all backgrounds have a right to tell their own stories. Marginalized populations have historically been shut out when it comes to creating art that reflects their own experiences. Even when someone else tells your story well, it is not the same as you personally having the freedom and the ability to teach the world about your own journey.

The most authentic story is told by the one who lived it.

Deedee Cummings – Author
As a therapist, attorney, author, and CEO of *Make A Way Media*, Deedee Cummings has spent more than two decades working within the family support field. Much of her writing is reflective of her experience working with kids in therapeutic foster care. All sixteen of Deedee's diverse picture books, poetry books, and workbooks are not only fun for kids and adults to read, they also work to teach coping skills, reinforce the universal message of love, encourage mindfulness, and facilitate inclusion for all. Deedee is an award-winning author whose work has appeared in national publications such as *Essence Magazine*, *USA Today*, *Forbes*, and the *Huffington Post*. Deedee resides in Louisville, Kentucky.

Charlene Mosley – Illustrator
Born in Berlin, Charlene Mosley is a fine artist, illustrator, and muralist, who works in oil and watercolor. Charlene has exhibited in both national and international exhibitions. In 2016, Charlene was one of the contributing artists of *Loving Vincent*, the first fully-painted, Oscar-nominated feature film. Mosley's current work discusses the 21st-century media-driven society and its relationship to technology and nature. She resides in San Diego.

In The Nick Of Time Too

Nick Saint and his best friend, Cooper, reunite in this warm holiday story about the magic of Christmas. A surprise visit leads to a journey of self-discovery and a deeper understanding of the true meaning of the holiday spirit.

Nick and Cooper receive a charge to spread kindness and hope in their everyday lives. Will Cooper listen to his friend and help Nick save the day again? Will you also be moved to action and accept Santa's challenge to spread kindness wherever you go?

Children of all ages and backgrounds will be inspired by this story and will understand that love, hope, and kindness come to us in many shapes and all colors.

Deedee Cummings

Cover Art Credit:
Charlene Mosley